THIS CANDLEWICK BOOK BELONGS TO:

_____

_____

_____

_____

For R. N. L.

Second U.S. edition 1995

Library of Congress Cataloging-in-Publication Data

Twelve days of Christmas (English folk song)
The twelve days of Christmas / illustrated by Louise Brierley.—2nd U.S. ed.
Summary: More and more gifts arrive from a young girl's true love
on each of the twelve days of Christmas.
ISBN 1-56402-525-X
1. Folk songs, English—England—Texts.   2. Christmas music.
[1. Folk songs—England.   2. Christmas music.]
I. Brierley, Louise, ill.   II. Title.
PZ8.3.T8517   1995
782.42'1723'0268—dc20   94-19705

2 4 6 8 10 9 7 5 3 1

Printed in Hong Kong

The pictures in this book were done in watercolor.

Candlewick Press
2067 Massachusetts Avenue
Cambridge, Massachusetts 02140

THE TWELVE DAYS OF
CHRISTMAS

illustrated by
LOUISE BRIERLEY

CANDLEWICK PRESS
CAMBRIDGE, MASSACHUSETTS

On the first day
of Christmas

My true love sent to me

A partridge in a pear tree.

On the second day
of Christmas

My true love sent to me

Two turtle doves,

And a partridge in a pear tree.

On the third day
of Christmas

My true love sent to me

Three French hens,

Two turtle doves,

And a partridge in a pear tree.

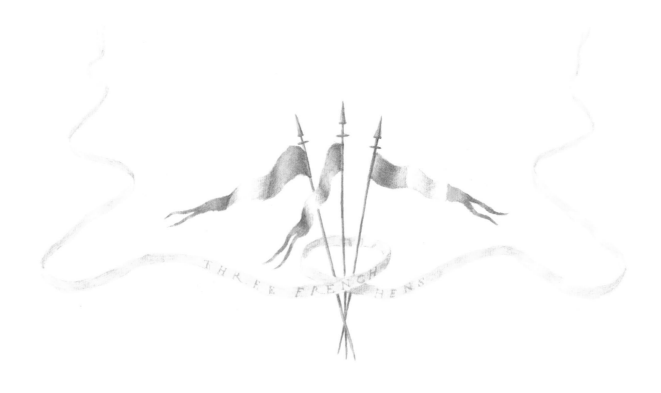

On the fourth day of Christmas

My true love sent to me

Four calling birds,

Three French hens,

Two turtle doves,

And a partridge in a pear tree.

On the fifth day
of Christmas

My true love sent to me

Five gold rings,

Four calling birds,

Three French hens,

Two turtle doves,

And a partridge in a pear tree.

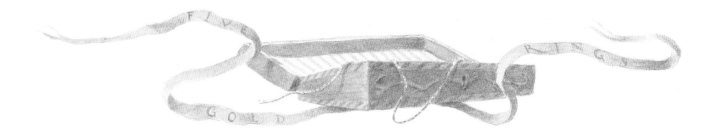

On the sixth day
of Christmas

My true love sent to me

Six geese a-laying,

Five gold rings,

Four calling birds,

Three French hens,

Two turtle doves,

And a partridge in a pear tree.

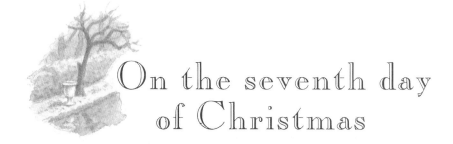

On the seventh day
of Christmas

My true love sent to me

Seven swans a-swimming,

Six geese a-laying,

Five gold rings,

Four calling birds,

Three French hens,

Two turtle doves,

And a partridge in a pear tree.

On the eighth day of Christmas

My true love sent to me

Eight maids a-milking,

Seven swans a-swimming,

Six geese a-laying,

Five gold rings,

Four calling birds,

Three French hens,

Two turtle doves,

And a partridge in a pear tree.

On the ninth day of Christmas

My true love sent to me

Nine drummers drumming,

Eight maids a-milking,

Seven swans a-swimming,

Six geese a-laying,

Five gold rings,

Four calling birds,

Three French hens,

Two turtle doves,

And a partridge in a pear tree.

On the tenth day of Christmas

My true love sent to me

Ten pipers piping,

Nine drummers drumming,

Eight maids a-milking,

Seven swans a-swimming,

Six geese a-laying,

Five gold rings,

Four calling birds,

Three French hens,

Two turtle doves,

And a partridge in a pear tree.

On the eleventh day of Christmas

My true love sent to me

Eleven ladies dancing,

Ten pipers piping,

Nine drummers drumming,

Eight maids a-milking,

Seven swans a-swimming,

Six geese a-laying,

Five gold rings,

Four calling birds,

Three French hens,

Two turtle doves,

And a partridge in a pear tree.

On the twelfth day of Christmas

My true love sent to me

Twelve lords a-leaping,

Eleven ladies dancing,

Ten pipers piping,

Nine drummers drumming,

Eight maids a-milking,

Seven swans a-swimming,

Six geese a-laying,

Five gold rings,

Four calling birds,

Three French hens,

Two turtle doves,

And a partridge in a pear tree.

TWELVE LORDS-A-LEAPING

LOUISE BRIERLEY has worked as a free-lance book and magazine illustrator since graduating from art school in 1983. She has lived in Germany, France, and England, and her paintings have been exhibited in several countries.